Contents

		page
Introduction		v
Chapter 1	How It All Began	1
Chapter 2	Halfway across America	4
Chapter 3	The Greatest Ride of My Life	6
Chapter 4	The Rocky Mountains	9
Chapter 5	Out on the Street	11
Chapter 6	The Cost of Living	14
Chapter 7	Love in LA	20
Chapter 8	Dean's Story	26
Chapter 9	On the Road Again	29
Chapter 10	Driving South	32
Chapter 11	Journey to San Francisco	38
Chapter 12	Goodbyes	42
Chapter 13	Back in San Francisco	44
Chapter 14	The Road Is Life	48
Chapter 15	Driving East	52
Chapter 16	Together Again in Denver	58
Chapter 17	Across the Rio Grande	62
Chapter 18	Mexico City	66
Chapter 19	The Last Goodbye	68
Activities		71

Introduction

But all the crazy things that were going to happen began then. It would mix up all my friends, and all I had left of my family, in a big dust cloud over the American Night.

Love, jazz, and wild times are all part of Sal Paradise's adventures in *On the Road*, the story of his travels across the United States with his strange friend Dean Moriarty, "the perfect guy for the road," and their crazy companions. Around the late 1940s it was common for rich people who wanted their cars to be driven long distances to look for drivers. These were people who were going to the same destination but did not have the money for plane, bus, or train tickets. The drivers then found passengers to share the cost of the gas. This gave a lot of young people, like Sal and Dean, the opportunity to travel.

Jack Kerouac was born in the north-east of the United States in 1922 and died in 1969 at the age of 47. He wrote his first novel at eleven and at seventeen he decided to become a writer. A year later he began traveling after reading about the life of Jack London, another famous North American who wrote about life in the great outdoors.

During his short life, Kerouac produced many novels, plays, and books of poetry. However, he is best known for his road novels of the fifties and sixties. *On the Road* (1957) is the most famous of these. Other works include *The Subterraneans* (1958), *The Dharma Bums* (1958), *Doctor Sax* (1959), and *Big Sur* (1962).

A number of real people lie behind the characters in *On the Road*. The fictional Dean Moriarty is Kerouac's real-life traveling companion, Neal Cassady; the poet Allen Ginsberg appears as Carlo Marx; and the writer William Burroughs is Old Bull Lee.

On the Road

JACK KEROUAC

Level 5

Retold by John Escott

Series Editor the ~~Hopkins~~ and Jocelyn Potter

Pearson Education Limited

Edinburgh Gate, Harlow,

Essex CM20 2JE, England

and Associated Companies throughout the world.

ISBN 0 582 40265 4

First published in the United States of America by the Viking Press, Inc. 1957
First published in Great Britain by André Deutsch 1958
Published by Penguin Books 1972
This edition first published 1999
Third impression 2000

Original copyright © Jack Kerouac 1955, 1957
Text copyright © Penguin Books 1999
All rights reserved

Typeset by Digital Type, London
Set in 11/14pt Bembo
Printed in Spain by Mateu Cromo, S. A. Pinto (Madrid)

Published by Pearson Education Limited in association with
Penguin Books Ltd, both companies being subsidiaries of Pearson Plc

For a complete list of the titles available in the Penguin Readers series please write to your local
Pearson Education office or to: Marketing Department, Penguin Longman Publishing,
5 Bentinck Street, London W1M 5RN.

Chapter 1 How It All Began

What you could call my life on the road began when I first met Dean Moriarty, not long after my wife and I separated. Before that, I often dreamed of going West to see the country, always planning but never going. Dean is the perfect guy for the road because he was actually born on the road, when his parents were passing through Salt Lake City in 1926, on their way to Los Angeles. First reports of him came to me through Chad King. Chad showed me some letters from Dean, written in a New Mexico jail for kids. This is all far back, when Dean was not the way he is today, when he was just a mysterious jail-kid. Then news came that Dean was out of jail and was coming to New York for the first time; also there was talk that he had just married a girl called Marylou.

One day in college Chad and Tim Gray told me Dean was staying in rooms in East Harlem. He had arrived the night before with beautiful little Marylou. They got off the Greyhound bus at 50th Street, went around the corner to Hector's cafe and bought beautiful big cream cakes.

All the time, Dean was telling Marylou things like: "Now, darling, here we are in New York and although I haven't quite told you everything I was thinking when we crossed the Missouri River, it's absolutely necessary now to postpone all those things concerning our personal love, and at once begin thinking of work-life plans ..." That was the way he talked in those early days.

I went to their little apartment with the boys, and Dean came to the door in his shorts. Dean had blue eyes, and a real Oklahoma accent. He had worked on Ed Wall's farm in Colorado before he married Marylou. She was a pretty blonde, with long

1

curly hair. She sat on the couch, her smoky blue eyes staring. But although she was a sweet little girl, she was stupid and could do horrible things.

That night we drank beer and talked until dawn, and in the morning while we sat around smoking in the gray light of a gloomy day, Dean got up nervously, and walked around, thinking. Then he decided Marylou could get some breakfast. Later, I went away.

During the next week, he told Chad King that he absolutely had to learn how to write; Chad said that I was a writer and he should come to me for advice. Then Dean had a fight with Marylou in their Hoboken apartment just across the Hudson River from New York and she was so angry that she went to the police and accused Dean of some false, crazy thing so that Dean had to run away from Hoboken. He came right out to Paterson, New Jersey, where I was living with my aunt, and one night while I was studying there was a knock on the door. And there was Dean in the dark hall, saying, "Hello, you remember me – Dean Moriarty? I've come to ask you to show me how to write."

"And where's Marylou?" I asked. And Dean said that she had gone back to Denver. So we went out to have a few beers because we couldn't talk like we wanted to talk in front of my aunt, who took one look at Dean and decided that he was a madman.

In the bar I told Dean, "You didn't come to me only to learn to be a writer, and anyway what do I really know about it except that you have to work and work at it."

And he said, "Yes, of course, I know exactly what you mean and in fact all those problems have come to my attention, and . . ." and on and on about things I didn't understand, and he didn't either. But we understood each other on other levels of madness, and I agreed that he could stay at my house till he found a job. And we agreed to go out West at some time. That was the winter of 1947.

One night we went to New York, and it was the night that Dean met Carlo Marx. They liked each other immediately, and from that moment on I did not see Dean as often as before. And I was a little sorry too.

But all the crazy things that were going to happen began then. It would mix up all my friends, and all I had left of my family, in a big dust cloud over the American Night. Carlo told Dean of Old Bull Lee, Elmer Hassel, Jane: Lee in Texas growing marijuana, Hassel in jail, Jane wandering on Times Square, full of drugs, with her baby girl in her arms, until somebody took her to Bellevue Hospital. And Dean told Carlo about people in the West like Tommy Snark, the card player, Big Ed Dunkel, his many girlfriends, sex parties, and other adventures.

Then the spring came, the great time of traveling, and everybody was getting ready to go on one trip or another. I was busy working on my novel. And when I was halfway, and after a trip down South with my aunt to visit my brother Rocco, I got ready to travel West for the very first time.

Dean left before me. Carlo and I went with him to the 34th Street Greyhound★ bus station. Dean was wearing a real Western business suit for his big trip back to Denver. It was blue, and he bought it in a store on Third Avenue for eleven dollars. He also had a small typewriter, and he said he was going to start writing as soon as he got a job and a room in Denver. We had a last meal together, then Dean got on a bus which said Chicago and went off into the night. I promised myself to go the same way soon.

And this was really the way that my whole road experience began, and the things that happened were amazing, and must be told.

★Greyhound: an American bus company.

3

Chapter 2   Halfway across America

In July 1947, I was ready to go to the West Coast. I had written half my book, and had about fifty dollars, when my friend Remi Boncœur wrote me a letter from San Francisco. He wanted me to come out and go with him on a round-the-world trip, working on a ship. He was living with a girl called Lee Ann, and he said she was a wonderful cook and "everything will be great!"

"The trip West will be good for you," my aunt said. "Just come back in one piece!"

It was an ordinary bus trip to Chicago, with crying babies and hot sun, and country people getting on at one Pennsylvania town after another. I arrived in Chicago early in the morning, got a room, and went to sleep all day.

That night I went to a club and listened to jazz music till dawn. Then the following afternoon, I got a bus to Joliet, Illinois, then started walking West. I had already spent half my money. It was a warm and beautiful day for hitch-hiking and my first ride was with a truck along Route 6, thirty miles into great green Illinois. About three in the afternoon, a woman stopped for me in a little car. She wanted somebody to help her drive to Iowa, and I was happy to help. She drove for the first few hours, then I did. I'm not a very good driver, but I drove through the rest of Illinois to Davenport, Iowa, through Rock Island, where for the first time in my life I saw the Mississippi River. I got out at Davenport. Here the lady was going to her Iowa home town by another route.

The sun was going down. I had a few cold beers and walked to the edge of town. All the men were driving home from work, and one gave me a ride up the hill and left me at a lonely crossroads. A few cars went by, but no trucks. Soon it was dark, and there were no lights in the Iowa countryside. In a minute, nobody would be able to see me. Then a man going back into Davenport took me back where I started from.

I went to sit in the bus station, and ate apple pie and ice cream; that's almost all I ate all the way across the country. I decided to get a bus to the edge of the town, but this time near the gas stations. And after two minutes, a big truck stopped for me. The driver was a big guy who paid hardly any attention to me, so I could rest quietly without talking. We stopped later and he slept for a few hours in the driving seat. I slept too. Then, at dawn, we were off again, and an hour later the smoke of Des Moines appeared over the fields. He had to eat his breakfast now and wanted to rest, so I went right on into Des Moines, about four miles. I got a ride with two boys from the University of Iowa, and it was strange sitting in their new, comfortable car as we drove smoothly into town.

I spent all day sleeping in a room at a small, gloomy old hotel near the railroad line. The bed was big and clean and hard. I woke up as the sun was getting red – and for about fifteen seconds I didn't know who I was! I was far away from home, tired from traveling, and in a cheap hotel room I'd never seen. I was halfway across America, at the dividing line between the East of my early life and the West of my future. And maybe that's why I truly forgot who I was, on that strange red afternoon.

But I had to get moving, so I picked up my bag and went to eat. I ate apple pie and ice cream again. There were beautiful girls everywhere I looked in Des Moines that afternoon, but I had no time now for thoughts like that. But I promised myself a good time in Denver. Carlo Marx was already in Denver; Dean was there; Chad King and Tim Gray were there; and there was mention of Ray Rawlins and his beautiful blond sister, Babe Rawlins; and two waitresses Dean knew, the Bettencourt sisters; and even Roland Major, my old college writing friend was there. So I rushed past the pretty girls – and the prettiest girls in the world live in Des Moines.

Chapter 3 The Greatest Ride of My Life

The greatest ride of my life came outside of the town of Gothenburg. A flatback★ truck came by, and six or seven boys were lying out on it. The drivers were two young blond farmers from Minnesota, and they were picking up everybody they saw on that road. They were a smiling, handsome pair of young men.

The truck stopped and I ran up to it. "Is there room?"

"Sure, jump on," they said. "There's room for everybody."

I jumped on and the truck drove off. I looked around at the others. There were two young farmer boys from North Dakota. Two city boys from Columbus, Ohio, who were hitch-hiking around the United States for the summer. A tall slim fellow from Montana. Finally there were Mississippi Gene and his young friend. Mississippi Gene was a little thirty-year-old dark guy who rode on trains around the country. His friend was a sixteen-year-old tall blond kid, who was quiet and seemed to be running away from something. He had a worried look. Both of them wore old clothes that had turned black from the smoke of the railroads and from sleeping on the ground.

"Where are you going?" Mississippi Gene asked me.

"Denver," I said.

"You got any money?" asked Montana Slim.

"No," I said. "Well, maybe enough for some whisky till I get to Denver. What about you?"

"I know where I can get some," he said.

"Where?" I said.

"Anywhere," he said. "You can always follow a man down a dark street and rob him, can't you?"

★ Flatback: a truck with a flat trailer and no walls; also called "flatbed."

"Yes, I guess you can," I said.

"I'll do it if I really need some money. I'm going to Montana to see my father. I'll have to get off this truck at Cheyenne. These crazy boys are going to Los Angeles."

"Straight?" I said.

"All the way," he said. "If you want to go to LA, you got a ride."

I thought about this, but decided that I'd get off at Cheyenne too, and hitch-hike south ninety miles to Denver.

I was glad when we stopped to eat. We all went into the restaurant and had hamburgers and coffee, while the two blond farmers from Minnesota ate enormous meals. They were brothers, and they took farm machines from Los Angeles to Minnesota. On their trip to the West Coast, when the truck was empty, they picked up everybody on the road.

When we got back to the truck it was almost dark. The drivers smoked cigarettes.

"I'm going to buy a bottle of whisky," I told them.

"OK," they said. "But hurry."

Montana Slim and the two city boys came with me. We wandered the streets of North Platte and found a place to buy whisky. They gave me some money, and I bought a bottle, then we went back to the truck.

It got dark quickly. We all had a drink, except the two Minnesota brothers. "We never drink," they said. But they drove fast, and we were soon looking southwest toward Denver, a few hundred miles away.

I was excited. "Whooppee!" I shouted.

We passed the bottle of whisky to each other, and the stars came out, and I felt good.

When we came to the town of Ogallala, the two Dakota boys decided to get off and look for work. We watched them disappear into the night. I had to buy more cigarettes. Gene and the blond boy followed me and I bought a packet for both of them, and they thanked me.

It was nearly midnight, and cold, and the stars were getting brighter. We were in Wyoming now. Mississippi Gene began to sing a song: "I've got a pretty little girl, she's sweet sixteen, she's the prettiest thing you've ever seen," repeating it with other lines about how far he'd been, and how he wished that he could get back to her.

I said, "Gene, that's the prettiest song."

We got to Cheyenne, and saw crowds of people moving along the streets, crowded bars, and bright lights.

"It's Wild West Week!" said Montana Slim.

He and I jumped off and said goodbye to the others. We watched the truck move slowly through the crowds and disappear into the night.

Chapter 4 The Rocky Mountains

Montana Slim and I began going to the bars. I had about seven dollars. We picked up two pretty girls, a pretty young blonde and a fat girl with black hair. They were moody and not very intelligent, but we wanted to make love to them. We took them to a nightclub which was already closing, and I spent five dollars on whiskies for them and beer for us. I was drunk, but I didn't care. Everything was great. I just wanted the little blonde. I put my arms around her and wanted to tell her. The nightclub closed and we all wandered out into the dusty streets. I looked up at the sky. The wonderful stars were still there, burning.

The girls wanted to go to the bus station, so we went there, but it was to meet a sailor who was waiting for them. He was the fat girl's cousin, and he had friends with him. The blonde wanted to go to her home, in Colorado, just south of Cheyenne. "I'll take you in a bus," I said.

"No," she said, then went on, "I want to go to New York. I'm tired of this. There's no place to go except Cheyenne, and there's nothing in Cheyenne."

"There's nothing in New York," I said.

She went to join the sailor and the others. Slim was sleeping on a seat. I sat down and told myself that I was stupid. "Why didn't I save my money?" I thought. "Why did I spend it all on that stupid girl?" I laid down on the seat with my bag for a pillow and went to sleep.

I woke up at eight o'clock in the morning with a big headache. Slim had gone – to Montana, I guess. And there in the blue air I saw for the first time, far away, the great snowy tops of the Rocky Mountains. And I knew that I had to get to Denver at once.

9

I got a ride in a car with a young fellow from Connecticut. He talked and talked. I was sick from drinking, and once I almost had to put my head out of the window. But by the time he let me off at Longmont, Colorado, I was feeling OK.

It was beautiful in Longmont. I slept for two hours under a big tree near a gas station, then got a ride with a Denver businessman. We had a long, warm conversation about life, all the way to Denver.

In those days I didn't know Dean as well as I do now, so I phoned Chad King's house. He came and picked me up in his old Ford car that he used for trips into the mountains. Chad is a slim blond boy, and he smiled when he saw me.

Chad had decided not to be Dean's friend any more, for some strange reason, and he didn't even know where he lived.

"Is Carlo Marx in town?" I asked.

"Yes," he said. But he wasn't talking to him any more either. It seemed that Chad King, Tim Gray, Roland Major, and the Rawlinses were not seeing or speaking with Dean Moriarty and Carlo Marx. And I was in the middle of this interesting war.

My first afternoon in Denver I slept in Chad King's room while Chad worked at the library, and in the evening his mother cooked us a wonderful dinner.

But where was Dean?

Chapter 5 Out on the Street

I went to live with Roland Major in a really nice apartment that belonged to Tim Gray's parents. We each had a bedroom, and there was a big living room where Major sat writing his short stories. He was a fat, red-faced hater of everything who could turn on the warmest and most charming smile in the world when he wanted to.

The Rawlinses lived near the apartment. This was a lovely family – a young mother, with five sons and two daughters. The wild son was Ray Rawlins, and one of Ray's sisters was a beautiful blonde called Babe. She was Tim Gray's girl. And Major's girl was Tim Gray's sister Betty. I was the only guy without a girl.

I asked everybody, "Where's Dean?" They smiled but said they didn't know.

Then it happened. The phone rang and it was Carlo Marx. He gave me the address of his apartment and I rushed over to meet him.

"Where's Dean?" I asked him.

"Dean's in Denver," he said. And he told me that Dean was making love to two girls at the same time. Marylou, his first wife, and Camille, a new girl.

Carlo and I went through the streets in the Denver night. The air was so soft, the stars so beautiful, the promise of every street so great, that I thought I was in a dream. We came to an old red-brick building and went up carpeted stairs. Carlo knocked, then moved back to hide. He didn't want Camille to see him. Dean opened the door. He had no clothes on. I saw a dark-haired girl on the bed, one beautiful creamy leg half-covered. She looked up.

11

"Sal!" said Dean. "You've arrived! You finally got on that old road. Now, Camille –" He turned toward her. "This is my old friend from New York. It's his first night in Denver and it's absolutely necessary for me to take him out and find him a girl."

"But what time will you be back?" she said.

"It is now –" He looked at his watch. "Exactly one-fourteen. I shall be back at exactly three-fourteen for our hour together, darling, and then, as you know, I have to go and see the one-legged lawyer – in the middle of the night, strange as it seems." (This was so that he could see Carlo later, who was still hiding.)

We rushed off into the night, and Carlo joined us downstairs.

"Sal, I have a girl waiting for you this very minute," said Dean. "A waitress, Rita Bettencourt, and I've just *got* to make love to her sister tonight. Tomorrow I know where I can find you a job in the Camargo markets."

We got to the house where the waitress sisters lived. The one for me was still working, but the sister that Dean wanted was in. We sat down on her couch. I was due to phone Ray Rawlins at this time, and I did. He came over at once, took off his shirt, and began putting his arms around Mary Bettencourt. Bottles rolled on the floor. We drank. Three o'clock came, and Dean rushed off for his hour with Camille. He was back soon, and the other sister came. We needed a car now, and Ray Rawlins phoned a friend who came with his. We all jumped in.

"Let's go to my apartment!" I shouted.

We did, and ran shouting into the building. Roland Major stopped us at the door. "I won't let you behave like this in Tim Gray's apartment!" he said.

"What?" we all shouted. Everything got confusing. Rawlins was rolling on the grass with one of the waitresses. Major was shouting, "You can't come in!" Then we all rushed back to the Denver bars and I was suddenly alone in the street with no money. My last dollar was gone.

I walked five miles up to Colfax to my comfortable bed in the apartment. Major had to let me in. The nights in Denver are cool, and I slept like a baby.

Chapter 6 The Cost of Living

I worked in the markets for one day, but I didn't go back. I had a bed, and Major bought food, and I did the cooking and washed the dishes. Then I got involved in a trip to the mountains and didn't see Dean and Carlo for five days. Babe Rawlins borrowed a car. We bought suits and drove to Central City, Ray Rawlins driving, Tim Gray sitting in the back, and Babe up front. Central City was an old town that was once called the Richest Square Mile in the World, because of the silver that could be found in the hills.

Babe Rawlins knew of an old house on the edge of the town where we could sleep for the weekend. All we had to do was clean it – which took all afternoon and part of the night, but we had plenty of beer so everything was OK.

We called out to girls who went by in the street. "Come and help us. Everybody's invited to our party tonight." They joined us, and soon the sun went down.

It was a wonderful night. Tim, Rawlins, and I went to a bar and had a few extra-big beers. There was a piano player in the bar, and beyond the back door was a view of the mountain in the moonlight. Later, we went back to our house and the girls were getting everything ready for the party. Soon great crowds of girls came in, and then we danced and sang and drank more beer. The place filled up. People brought bottles. The night got more and more exciting. "I wish Dean and Carlo were here," I thought.

There were beds in the other rooms, and I was sitting on one talking to a girl. Suddenly, there was a great crowd of teenage boys rushing in. They were drunk, and they spoiled our party. After five minutes, every girl left with one or the other of them. Ray, Tim, and I decided to go back to the bars. Major was gone, Babe and Betty were gone.

14

There was some kind of tourist from Argentina in one place, and he got annoyed when Ray gave him a push to make room at the bar. Ray gave me his glass and knocked him down. There were screams, and Tim and I pulled Ray out. We went to other bars, and much later we rolled back to the house and went to sleep.

In the morning I woke up and turned over. A big cloud of dust rose from the bed. I tried to open the window, but it wouldn't open. Tim Gray was in the bed too, and we started coughing. Our breakfast was stale beer. Babe came from her hotel and we got our things together, ready to leave. Suddenly, everything seemed to be going wrong. As we were going out to the car, Babe slipped and fell flat on her face. We helped her up and got in the car. Major and Betty joined us, and it was a sad ride back to Denver.

My time there was coming to an end, but I had no money. I sent my aunt an airmail letter asking her for fifty dollars. "It will be the last money I ask you for," I wrote. "You will get it back as soon as I get work on that ship." The money arrived two days later, and I bought a bus ticket for San Francisco, spending half the fifty. In a last phone call, Dean said he and Carlo might join me on the West Coast.

I was two weeks late meeting Remi Boncœur in San Francisco. There was a note pinned on the door of his house: *Sal Paradise! If nobody is home, climb in through the window. Signed Remi Boncœur.*

Remi was asleep, but he woke up and saw me come in through the window. "Where have you been, Paradise?" he said. "You're two weeks late!" He slapped me on the back, hit Lee Ann, his girl, on the chest, laughed and cried and screamed, "Oh, Paradise! The one and only Paradise! Did you see, Lee Ann? He came in through the window!"

I soon discovered that Lee Ann had a cruel tongue and said bad things to Remi every day. They spent all week saving pennies and went out on Saturdays to spend fifty dollars in three hours. Remi slept with Lee Ann in the bed across the room, and I slept on a couch by the window.

"You must not touch Lee Ann," Remi told me. "I don't want to find you two kissing and making love when you think I'm not looking." I looked at Lee Ann. She was a pretty, honey-colored girl, but there was hate in her eyes for both of us.

Remi was working as a guard at the barracks, and he got me a similar job. The barracks were the temporary home of building workers who were going overseas. They stayed there, waiting for their ship. Most of them were on their way to Okinawa, Japan. And most of them were running away from something – usually the law.

One night I was the only guard in the barracks for six hours. Everybody seemed to be drunk that night. It was because their ship was leaving in the morning. I tried to get them quiet, but I finally gave in and had a drink with them. Soon I was as drunk as anybody else.

I earned fifty-five dollars a week and sent my aunt forty. Some nights Remi and I were working together and Remi tried all the doors, hoping to find one unlocked.

"Why do you have to steal all the time?" I asked him.

"The world owes me a few things, that's all," he said.

When we got to the barracks kitchen, we looked around to check that nobody was there. Remi opened a window and climbed through, and I followed him. We looked in the refrigerators to see what we could take home in our pockets. One night I waited a long time as he filled a box with cans and other food. Then we couldn't get it through the window and Remi had to put it all back. Later that night, he found a key to the kitchen and went back and filled the box again.

"Paradise," Remi said, "I have told you several times what the President said: 'We must cut the cost of living.'"

There was an old rusty ship near the shore, and Remi wanted to row out to it. So one afternoon Lee Ann packed a lunch and we hired a boat and went out. I watched Lee Ann take all her clothes off and lie down in the sun, then Remi and I went down to the engine rooms, and began looking for anything valuable, but there was nothing there.

"I'd love to sleep in this old ship one night when the fog comes in," I said.

Remi was amazed. "Sal, don't you realize there may be the ghosts of old sea captains on this thing? But I'll pay you five dollars if you're brave enough to do it."

"OK!" I said. Remi ran to tell Lee Ann. I went too, but I tried not to look at her.

♦

I wrote long letters to Dean and Carlo, who were now staying with Old Bull Lee in Texas. And everything began to go wrong with Remi and Lee Ann and me. Remi flew down to Hollywood with something I had written, but he couldn't get anybody interested in it and he flew back. Then he saved all his money, about a hundred dollars, and took Lee Ann and me to the races at Golden Gate, near Richmond. He put twenty dollar bets on to win, but before the seventh race he was broke. We had to hitch-hike back to San Francisco.

We had no money, and that night it started raining. Lee Ann was angry with both of us. She was sure that we were hiding money from her. She threatened to leave Remi.

"Where will you go?" asked Remi.

"To Jimmy," she said.

"Jimmy!" said Remi. "A clerk at the races! Did you hear that, Sal?"

"Get out!" she told Remi. "Pack your things and get out."

Remi started packing, and I imagined myself all alone in this rainy house with that angry young woman. Then Remi pushed Lee Ann and she began screaming. She put on her raincoat and went out to find a cop. She didn't find one and came back all wet, while I hid in my corner with my head between my knees. "What am I doing three thousand miles from home?" I thought. "Why did I come here?"

"And another thing, you dirty man," shouted Lee Ann. "Tonight was the last night I cook for you so that you can fill your stomach and get fat and rude in front of my eyes."

"I'm very disappointed in both of you," said Remi. "I flew to Hollywood, I got Sal a job, I bought you beautiful dresses, Lee Ann. Now I ask only one thing. My father is coming to San Francisco next Saturday night. Will you come with me and pretend that you, Lee Ann, are my girl, and that you, Sal, are my friend? I've arranged to borrow a hundred dollars for Saturday night. I want my father to have a good time, and go away without any reason to worry about me."

This surprised me. Remi's father was a doctor. "A hundred dollars! He's got more money than you will ever have!" I said to Remi. "You'll be in debt, man!"

"That's all right," he said quietly. "He's coming with his young wife. We must be very pleasant and polite."

Lee Ann was impressed, and looked forward to Saturday.

I had finished my job at the barracks and this was going to be my last Saturday night. Remi and Lee Ann went to meet his father at the hotel room first. I got drunk in the bar downstairs, then went up to join them all very late. I said something loud in bad French to Dr. Boncœur, and Remi got angry and embarrassed.

We all went to an expensive restaurant where poor Remi spent at least fifty dollars for the five of us. And now the worst thing happened. My old friend Roland Major was sitting in the restaurant bar! He had just arrived from Denver and had a job on a San Francisco newspaper. He was drunk. He came over, slapped me on the back, and threw himself into the seat next to Dr. Boncœur.

Remi had an embarrassed red face. "Please introduce your friend, Sal," he said.

"Roland Major of the San Francisco *Argus*," I said, trying not to laugh. Lee Ann was very angry with me.

Major began chatting in Dr. Boncœur's ear. "How do you like teaching high-school French?" he shouted.

"Excuse me, but I don't teach high-school French," said Boncœur.

Major knew that he was being rude, but didn't care. I got drunk and began to talk nonsense to the doctor's young wife. I drank a lot, and had to go to the men's room every two minutes. "Everything is going wrong," I thought. "Here I am at the end of America – no more land – and nowhere to go except back. But I'll go to Hollywood, and back through Texas and see my old friends."

In the morning, while Remi and Lee Ann were asleep, I decided to leave. I quietly climbed out of the window, and left with my bag.

And I never did spend the night at that old ghost ship.

Chapter 7 Love in LA

Two rides took me to the south side of Bakersfield, and then my adventure began. I stood for two hours on the side of the road, as cars rushed by toward Los Angeles. None of them stopped, and at midnight I began walking back into the town. I was going to have to spend two dollars or more for a bus ticket to LA, so I went to the bus station.

I was waiting for the LA bus when I suddenly saw the prettiest little Mexican girl. She was in one of the buses that came in for a rest stop. Her hair was long and black, and her eyes were great big blue things. I wished that I was on her bus, and felt a pain like a knife in my heart, the way I did every time I saw a girl that I loved going in the opposite direction in this too-big world.

Some time later, I picked up my bag and got on the LA bus. And who was sitting there, alone? It was the Mexican girl! I sat opposite her and began planning immediately. I was so lonely, so sad, so tired, so broken, that I found the courage to talk to her. "Miss, would you like to use my raincoat for a pillow?"

She looked up with a smile. "No, thank you," she said.

I sat back, shaking, and lit a cigarette. I waited till she looked at me, with a sad little look of love, and I got up and went over to her. "May I sit with you, miss?" I said.

"If you want to," she said.

And I did. "Where are you going?"

"LA," she said, and I loved the way she said it. I love the way everybody says "LA" on the Coast; but then, it's their one and only golden town.

"That's where I'm going too," I said.

We sat and told each other our stories. Her story was this: she had a husband and a child. Her husband beat her, so she left him,

20

and was going to LA to live with her sister for a while. She had left her little son with her family.

We talked and talked, and I wanted to put my arms around her. She said she loved to talk with me, and without saying anything about it, we began to hold hands. And in the same way it was silently and beautifully decided that when I got to my hotel room in LA, she would be beside me. I ached all over for her, and I rested my head in her beautiful hair.

"I love love," she said, closing her eyes, and I promised her beautiful love.

The bus arrived in Hollywood, in the gray, dirty dawn, and she slept in my arms. We got off at Main Street, and here my mind went crazy. I don't know why. I began to imagine that Terry – that was her name – was a girl who tricked men and took them to a hotel, where one of her friends waited with a gun. But I never told her this.

The first hotel we saw had a vacant room, and soon I was locking the door behind me and she was sitting on the bed taking off her red shoes. I kissed her gently, then went out and got some whisky. Terry was in the bathroom when I got back. I poured whisky into one big water glass, and we started to drink.

"I know a girl called Dorie," I told her. "She's six foot tall and has red hair. If you come to New York, she will show you where to find work."

"Who is this Dorie?" she said, suspecting something bad. "Why do you tell me about her?" She began to get drunk in the bathroom.

"It doesn't matter. Come on to bed," I said.

"Six foot, and with red hair?" she screamed. "And I thought you were a nice college boy! But you're a man who employs prostitutes!"

"No! Listen, Terry!" I cried. "It's not true! Please, listen to me and understand, I'm not like that!" And then I got angry. "Why am

I begging a stupid little Mexican girl to believe me?" I shouted. And I picked up her red shoes and threw them at the bathroom door. "Get out!" Then I took off my clothes and went to bed.

Terry came out of the bathroom with tears in her eyes, saying "Sorry! I'm sorry!" Her simple and strange little mind had decided that the kind of man who employs prostitutes does not throw shoes at doors. Sweetly and silently she took off her clothes and slid her little body into bed next to mine. I made love to her, and then we fell asleep and slept until late afternoon.

We were together for the next fifteen days. We decided to hitch-hike to New York together; and she was going to be my girl. Terry wanted to start at once with the twenty dollars I had left. I didn't like it. Like a fool, I considered the problem for two days, and my twenty was soon ten. But we were very happy in our little hotel room.

LA is the loneliest city in America; New York gets ice cold in the winter, but it's a friendlier city. South Main Street, LA, where Terry and I walked sometimes, was full of lights and wildness. Cops stopped and searched people on almost every corner. You could smell beer and marijuana in the air. All the cops in LA were handsome, and were hoping to get into Hollywood movies. Everyone came to get into Hollywood movies, even me. Terry and I tried to get work, but failed. We still had ten dollars.

"I'm going to get my clothes from my sister and we'll hitch-hike to New York," said Terry. "Come on, let's do it." So we hurried to her sister's house, somewhere out beyond Alameda Avenue. I waited in a dark street behind some Mexican kitchens because Terry didn't want her sister to see me. I could hear Terry and her sister arguing in the soft, warm night. I was ready for anything.

Terry came out and took me to an apartment house in Central Avenue. And what a wild place that is. We went up dirty stairs and came to the room of Terry's friend, Margarina, who owed Terry a skirt and a pair of shoes. Terry got her clothes, then we went out on to the street and a black guy whispered "marijuana" into my ear. "One dollar," and I said OK, bring it.

So we went back to the hotel room and smoked the little brown cigarette – but nothing happened. It wasn't marijuana at all! I wished that I was wiser with my money.

Terry and I decided to hitch-hike to New York with the rest of our money. She got five dollars from her sister that night. Now we had about thirteen dollars. We got a ride in a red car to Arcadia, California, then walked several miles down the road and stood under a road lamp. Suddenly, cars full of young kids went by. They laughed and shouted at us, and I hated every one of them. "Who do they think they are, shouting at somebody on the road?" I thought. "Just because their parents can afford roast beef on Sundays." And we didn't get a ride.

That night, in a little four-dollar hotel room, we held each other tight and made a plan. Next morning we were going to get a bus to Bakersfield and get a job picking grapes. We could live in a tent. After a few weeks of that, we could go to New York the easy way, by bus.

But there were no jobs in Bakersfield. We ate a Chinese dinner, then went across the railroad lines to the Mexican part of town where Terry talked with the Mexicans, asking for jobs. It was night now, and the little Mexican street was bright with the lights of movie theaters, cafes, and bars. Terry talked to everybody, then we bought a bottle of whisky and went and sat near the railroad buildings. We sat and drank till midnight, then got up and walked to the highway.

Terry had a new idea. "We can hitch-hike to my home town, Sabinal, and live in my brother's garage," she said.

We got a ride in a truck and arrived in Sabinal just before dawn. I took her to an old hotel by the railroad and we went to bed comfortably.

In the bright, sunny morning Terry got up early and went to find her brother. I slept till noon. Terry arrived with her brother, his friend, and her child. Her brother's name was Rickey. He was a wild Mexican guy who liked whisky, and he had a car. His friend, Ponzo, was a big fat Mexican who spoke English without much accent. I could see that he liked Terry. Her little boy was Johnny, seven years old, with dark eyes, and a sweet kid.

"Today we drink, tomorrow we work!" Rickey said. And off we went to a bar. It was a noisy place, and soon we were drinking and shouting with the music while little Johnny played with other kids. The sun began to get red, and we came out and got into the car again. Off we went to a highway bar, and later I spent a dollar on a meal for Terry and me in a Mexican restaurant. Now I had four dollars.

Rickey was drunk and poor little Johnny was asleep on my arm as we drove back toward Sabinal. That night, Terry and Johnny and I slept in a place with rooms for rent and tents out at the back. We had a room. Rickey drove on to sleep at his father's house, and Ponzo went to find his truck to sleep in.

In the morning I got up and went for a short walk. We were five miles outside of Sabinal, in cotton and grape-picking country. I asked the woman who owned the place, "Are any of the tents vacant?" and she said there was one. It was the cheapest – a dollar a day. I gave her a dollar and we moved into it.

Later I went to look for some cotton-picking work, and got a job with one of the farmers. He gave me a big sack and told me to start at dawn the next day. On the way back, some grapes fell off the back of a truck, and I picked them up and took them back for Terry and Johnny.

"Johnny and I will help you pick cotton," Terry told me. "I'll show you how to do it. It's hard work."

She was right. Picking cotton was hard work, and after an hour the next day my fingers began to bleed and my back began

24

to ache. But it was beautiful country. Across the fields were the tents, and beyond them the brown cotton fields; and beyond them the snow-topped Sierra Mountains in the blue morning air.

Johnny and Terry arrived at noon to help me. And little Johnny was faster than I was! And, of course, Terry was twice as fast. We worked together all afternoon, and when the sun got red we went back with my sack. The farmer weighed it – and gave me one-and-a-half dollars. Then I borrowed a bicycle from one of the other men and rode down to a highway store and bought bread, butter, coffee, and cake. On the way back, traffic going to LA and San Francisco almost knocked me off my bicycle, and I swore and swore. I looked up into the dark sky and prayed to God for a better life and a better chance to do something for the little people I loved. But nobody was listening.

Every day I earned less than two dollars. It was just enough to buy food in the evening. Time went by, and I forgot about Dean and Carlo and the road. Johnny and I played all the time, and Terry mended clothes. It was October now, and the nights were colder. Finally, we did not have enough money to pay the rent for the tent.

"We have to leave here," I said. "Go back to your family, Terry. You can't live in tents with a baby like Johnny, the poor little thing is cold. And I have to get to New York."

"I want to go with you, Sal," she said.

"But how?"

"I don't know," she said. "But I'll miss you. I love you."

"But I have to leave," I said.

"Yes, yes. We lay down one more time, then you leave," she said.

So we made love one more time.

Chapter 8 Dean's Story

Times Square in New York.

I had traveled eight thousand miles around America and I was back in Times Square. Paterson, where my aunt lives, is a few miles from Times Square. I had no money to go home in the bus, but I finally begged the price of a ticket from a Greek guy.

When I got home, I ate nearly everything in the refrigerator.

My aunt looked at me. "Poor little Salvatore," she said in Italian. "You're thin. Where have you been all this time?"

I couldn't sleep that night, I just smoked in bed. The half-finished book I had been writing was on the desk. It was October. Everybody goes home in October.

It was more than a year before I saw Dean again. I stayed home all that time, finished my book and began going to college. At Christmas 1948 my aunt and I went down to visit my brother in Virginia. I had been writing to Dean and he told me he was coming East again. I told him I was going to be in Testament, Virginia, between Christmas and New Year.

One day when all our relations were sitting in the house and talking, a 1949 Hudson car stopped outside. There was mud and dust on it. A tired young fellow got out, came to the door, and rang the bell. He was wearing a torn shirt and he needed a shave. I suddenly realized it was Dean! He had come all the way from San Francisco, and there were two more people sleeping in the car.

"Dean!" I cried, smiling. "It's you! And who's in the car?"

"Hello, hello, man!" he said. "It's Marylou and Ed Dunkel. We need a place to wash, and we're tired."

"But how did you get here so fast?" I said.

"Man, that Hudson goes fast!" he said.

"Where did you get it?" I asked.

"I bought it. I've worked on the railroads, for four hundred dollars a month."

For the next hour, my Southern relations did not know what was happening. They did not know who Dean, Marylou, or Ed Dunkel were, and they just sat and stared. There were now eleven people in that little house. Also, my brother Rocco had decided to move, and half his furniture had gone. He and his wife and baby were moving closer to the town of Testament. They had bought new furniture, and some of their old furniture was going to my aunt's house in Paterson, although we had not yet decided how it was going to get there. When Dean heard this he immediately offered to take it in the Hudson. He and I could carry the furniture to Paterson in two fast trips and bring my aunt back at the end of the second trip. This was going to save a lot of money, so it was agreed. Then Rocco's wife made a meal and we all sat down to eat.

I learned that Dean had lived happily with Camille in San Francisco since that fall in 1947; he had got a job on the railroad and earned a lot of money. He was also the father of a pretty little girl, Amy Moriarty. Then he suddenly went crazy while walking down the street one day. He saw a 1949 Hudson for sale and rushed to the bank for all his money. He bought the car immediately. Ed Dunkel was with him. Now they were broke.

Dean calmed Camille's fears. "I'm going to New York and bring Sal back," he told her. "I'll be back in a month."

She wasn't very pleased. "But why?" she asked. "Why are you doing this to me?"

He told her why, but of course it did not make sense.

Big, tall Ed Dunkel also worked on the railroad, and he met a girl called Galatea. He and Dean decided to bring the girl East and get her to pay for the meals and gas, but she wouldn't do this unless Ed married her. So he did. And a few days before Christmas they rolled out of San Francisco at seventy miles an hour. All the way, Galatea complained that she was tired and

27

wanted to sleep in a hotel. Two nights she forced them to stop and they spent money on hotel rooms. By the time they got to Tucson she was broke, and Dean and Ed managed to lose her in the hotel and traveled on alone.

Dean was driving through Las Cruces, New Mexico, when he suddenly wanted to see his first wife, Marylou, again. She was in Denver. He turned north and got to Denver in the evening. He found Marylou in a hotel. They made love for ten wild hours, and decided that they were going to be together again. She understood Dean. She knew that he was mad.

Dean, Marylou, and Ed Dunkel then left Denver and drove fast to my brother's house. They were hungry, and now they were eating everything they could see on my brother's table. Dean, with a sandwich in his hand, was dancing while he listened to jazz music on the radio. My Southern relations watched, amazed, but Dean paid no attention to them. He was different, I decided. He was crazier now.

Later, Dean, Marylou, Dunkel, and I went for a short ride in the Hudson. Dean was driving.

"What happened to Carlo?" he asked. "We must go and see Carlo tomorrow, darlings. Now, Marylou, we need some bread and meat to make a lunch for New York. How much money do you have, Sal? We'll put everything in the back seat – Mrs P's furniture – and all of us will sit up front, nice and close, and tell stories as we ride to New York!"

"I was enjoying a quiet Christmas in the country," I thought when we got back to the house and I saw the Christmas tree. "Now Dean Moriarty is here, and I'm off on the road again."

Chapter 9   On the Road Again

We packed my brother's furniture in the back of the car and promised to be back in thirty hours – thirty hours for a thousand miles north and south! In the large and comfortable Hudson there was plenty of room for all of us to sit up front. It was a new car, but the heater wasn't working, so a blanket covered our legs. We rushed through Richmond, Washington, Baltimore, and up to Philadelphia on a country road – and talked and talked. I told Dean and Marylou about a beautiful Italian girl with honey-colored hair called Lucille. "I met her at college," I said, "and I want to marry her." Marylou wanted to meet her.

In Philadelphia we went to a cafe and ate hamburgers. It was 3 a.m., and the cafe owner heard us talking about money. He offered to give us the hamburgers free, plus more coffee, if we washed all the dirty dishes in the kitchen. "OK!" we said.

Ed and I did the dishes while Dean and Marylou kissed and whispered together in a corner of the kitchen. We finished the dishes in fifteen minutes.

When dawn came we were driving through New Jersey, with the city of New York in the snowy distance. Then we went through the Lincoln Tunnel and over to Times Square, because Marylou wanted to see it.

After that, we went to my house in Paterson and slept. I was the first to wake up, late in the afternoon. There was a phone call from Old Bull Lee, who was in New Orleans. He was complaining.

"A girl called Galatea just arrived at my house," he said. "She's looking for a guy called Ed Dunkel."

"Tell her that Dunkel is with Dean and me," I said. "Tell her we'll probably pick her up in New Orleans on our way to the West Coast."

Then Galatea Dunkel came to the phone herself. "How is Ed?" she wanted to know. "Is he OK? Is he happy?"

I told her that he was. "How did you get from Tucson to New Orleans?" I asked.

"I wrote home for some money, and then got on a bus," she said. She was determined to catch up with Ed because she loved him. After the phone call, I told Big Ed. He sat in the chair and looked worried.

Next there was a call from Camille in San Francisco, and Dean talked to her. Then we phoned Carlo Marx at his home in Long Island and told him to come over. He arrived two hours later, and sat quietly watching Dean and me get ready for our trip alone to Virginia, to pick up the rest of the furniture and bring my aunt back.

Dean had a shower while I cooked some rice. Marylou mended his socks, and then we were ready to go. Dean, Carlo, and I drove into New York. We promised to see Carlo in thirty hours, in time to greet the New Year.

Dean talked all night. He was very excited about everything he saw, every detail of every moment that passed. "Everything is fine, Sal," he said. "God exists! I used to be a jail-kid, stealing cars. But all my jail-problems are over now. I shall never be in jail again." We passed a kid who was throwing stones at cars in the road. "Look," said Dean. "One day he'll throw a stone at a car, and the car will crash, and the man will die – all because of that little kid. Yes, God exists. And we know America. We're at home. I know the people. I know what they do."

There was nothing clear about the things he said, but what he *meant* to say was somehow pure and clear. Even my aunt listened, half curiously, as we drove back to New York that night, with the furniture in the back of the car.

At 4 a.m., in Washington, Dean stopped and phoned Camille in San Francisco. Soon after this, a police car overtook us and stopped us because we were going "too fast," although we were only doing thirty miles an hour. Dean and I went to the police station and tried to explain that we didn't have any money to pay the fifteen-dollar fine. But while we were arguing with the cops, one of them went out to look in the back of the car where my aunt was sleeping. She woke up and saw him.

"Don't worry," she said. "I don't have a gun. Search the car, if you want to. I'm going home with my nephew, and we didn't steal this furniture."

My aunt paid the fine, and Dean promised to pay her when he had the money (and he did, a year and a half later). We arrived at the house in Paterson at 8 a.m.

Chapter 10 Driving South

The New Year weekend went on for three days and three nights. Great gangs got into the Hudson and we slid through the snowy New York streets from party to party.

Lucille saw me with Dean and Marylou and she was not happy. "I don't like you when you're with them," she said.

Then Marylou began making love to me; she said Dean was going to stay with Camille and she wanted me to go with her. "Come back to San Francisco with us," she said. "We'll live together. I'll be a good girl for you." But I knew Dean loved Marylou, and I also knew Marylou was doing this to make Lucille jealous. And when Lucille saw Marylou pushing me into corners and kissing me, she accepted Dean's invitation to go out in the car; but they just talked and drank some whisky. Everything was mixed up.

"Lucille will never understand me," I thought, "because I like too many things and get all confused running from one falling star to another. I have nothing to offer anyone except my own confused thoughts."

The parties were enormous; there were at least a hundred people at one apartment. Something was happening in every corner, on every bed, and on every couch – not sex, just a New Year's party with wild screaming and wild radio music. Outside there was a wonderful snowstorm.

Ed Dunkel met Lucille's sister, and disappeared with her. And at five o'clock in the morning we were all climbing through the window of another apartment and another party. At dawn we were back in the first apartment, and I slept on a couch with a girl called Mona in my arms.

In the middle of the long, mad weekend, Dean and I went to

see the jazz piano player, George Shearing, at Birdland. These were his great 1949 days. When he finished playing the sweetest jazz I ever heard, Dean pointed at the empty piano seat and said, "God's empty chair." We were smoking marijuana, and it made me think that everything was about to arrive – the moment when you know everything, and everything is decided for ever.

I left everybody and went home to rest. My aunt said that I was wasting my time going around with Dean and his gang. But I knew that I wanted to go on one more wonderful trip to the West Coast and get back in time for the spring term at college.

We got ready to cross the country again. I gave Dean eighteen dollars to send to his wife; she was waiting for him to come home, and she was broke. What was Marylou thinking? I don't know. Ed Dunkel, as usual, just followed.

We phoned Old Bull Lee in New Orleans.

"What do you boys expect me to do with this Galatea Dunkel?" he complained. "She's been here two weeks now, hiding in her room and refusing to talk."

Ed spoke to him and promised to come.

I said goodbye to my aunt and promised to be back in two weeks.

◆

He was excited. "Whooee!" shouted Dean. "Here we go!"

From the dirty snows of New York to the green and river smells of New Orleans at the bottom of America; then west. Ed was in the back seat. Marylou, Dean, and I sat in the front, with Dean driving – fast.

"Now listen, Marylou, honey," he said. "In San Francisco we must go on living together. I know just the place for you, and I'll be home just a little less than every two days, for twelve hours. And you know what we can do in twelve hours, darling. I'll go on living at Camille's, and she won't know about us. We can do it, we did it before."

It was all right with Marylou, but I had understood that she would come to me in San Francisco. Now I began to see that they were going to stay together and I was going to be alone in California. But why think about that when all the golden land's in front of you, and all kinds of nice surprises wait for you?

We arrived in Washington at dawn, then Dean went to sleep in the back seat and Dunkel drove. We told him not to go too fast, but as soon as we were asleep he pushed the speed up to eighty, and a cop came after us and stopped us. He told us to follow him to the police station.

The cop at the police station didn't like Dean.

"The fine is twenty-five dollars," he said.

"But we only have forty dollars to go all the way to the Coast," said Dean.

"The fine is still twenty-five," said the cop. "And if you get another fine in Virginia you'll lose your car."

We paid the twenty-five dollars and drove away silently. But when we got through Richmond we began to forget about it, and everything was OK again.

I drove through South Carolina and beyond Macon, Georgia, while Dean, Marylou, and Ed slept. All alone in the night I had my own thoughts. "What am I doing? Where am I going?" I got very tired after Macon, and I woke Dean. We got out of the car for air, and suddenly we could smell grass and feel warm air on our faces. "We're in the South!" said Dean, laughing. "We left the winter behind!"

Ten miles down the road Dean drove into a gas station with the engine off. The man at the desk was asleep, and Dean jumped out quietly and put gas in the car before we drove off again.

I slept and woke up to hear music, and Dean and Marylou talking. We stopped at another gas station later, where Dunkel stole three packets of cigarettes. Then, suddenly, we could see New Orleans in the night in front of us.

The air in New Orleans was sweet, and you could smell the river. Dean was pointing at the women.

"Oh, I love, love, love women!" he shouted. "I think women are wonderful!"

We took the car on to the Algiers ferry to cross the Mississippi River, and jumped out to look at the brown water rolling by. We were leaving New Orleans behind on one side, and we could see sleepy Algiers on the other.

We came off the ferry and went to Old Bull Lee's house outside town. It was on a road that went across a muddy field. The house was old and the grass outside was knee-high. We stopped the car and I got out and went to the door. Jane Lee was standing there.

"Jane," I said. "It's me. It's us."

She knew that. "Yes," she said. "Bull isn't here."

"Is Galatea Dunkel here?"

Jane used to live with my wife and me in New York. Her face was thin and red, and she looked tired. Dean and the gang came out of the car, and then Galatea came from the back of the house to meet Ed. She was a serious girl, and her face was pale. Ed pushed a hand through his hair and said hello. She looked at him.

"Why did you do this to me?" she said.

She looked nastily at Dean, but he paid no attention to her. He asked Jane, "Is there anything to eat?"

It began to get confused then. Poor Bull came home and found his house full of crazy people, but he greeted me with a nice smile. He and his wife had two wonderful children. Dodie, eight years old; and little Ray, one year old. Ray ran around the yard without his clothes.

"Sal, you finally got here!" said Bull. "Let's go into the house and have a drink."

35

Bull was a teacher; a gray, quiet fellow that you didn't notice on the street unless you looked closer and saw his mad, bony head and strangely young face. He once studied medicine in Vienna; now he was studying things in the streets of life and the night.

He sat in his chair and Jane brought drinks.

"Sal, what kind of a person is this Ed Dunkel?" Bull asked. At that moment Ed was making Galatea forgive him, in the bedroom; it didn't take him long. We didn't know what to tell Bull about Ed.

Jane was never more than ten feet away from Bull, and she never missed a word that he said. Dean and I wanted Bull to take us to New Orleans.

"It's a very dull town," he said. But he agreed to take us. We left Jane with the children, and Dean drove us into New Orleans. He drove very fast, as usual, and Bull said, "You'll never get to California alive with this madman, Sal."

There was fog when we got to the ferry, and the lights of New Orleans were orange-bright across the brown water of the Mississippi. And a strange thing happened on the ferry that night. A girl threw herself over the side and drowned – either just before or just after our trip. We read about it in the newspaper the next day.

Old Bull took us to all the dull bars in the French Quarter, and we went back home at midnight. That night, Marylou took all the drugs that Bull would give her, and Ed went to lie with Galatea in the big bed that Old Bull and Jane never used. Dean was smoking marijuana.

I went for a walk by the Mississippi River.

Next day I got up early, and found Old Bull and Dean in the back yard. It was a lovely warm morning. Great beautiful clouds floated across the sky, and the softest wind blew in from the river.

We spent a mad day in downtown New Orleans, walking

around with the Dunkels. Dean was crazy that day. He and I and Ed Dunkel ran across the railroad line and jumped on a moving train while Marylou and Galatea waited in the car. We rode for half a mile, and Dean and Ed showed me the proper way to get off a moving train. We got back to the girls an hour late and of course they were angry.

Ed and Galatea decided to get a room in New Orleans and stay there and work. This was OK with Bull, who was tired of the whole gang now. We were waiting for some money to come from my aunt. When it came, the three of us – Dean, Marylou, and I – said goodbye.

We were off to California.

Chapter 11 Journey to San Francisco

We went back across the river on the ferry, then on a highway to Baton Rouge in purple darkness; turned west there, and crossed the Mississippi at a place called Port Allen. On through Louisiana – Lawtell, Eunice, Kinder, De Quincy, and Sabine. We had hardly enough money to get to San Francisco.

Soon we were crossing the Sabine River and saw lights in front of us. "Texas! It's Texas! Beaumont oil town!" We went through Beaumont, over the Trinity River, and on into Houston. The streets were empty at four o'clock in the morning.

Beyond Houston, Dean got tired and I drove. Rain began to fall. I drove through a little cow-town with a muddy main street, but couldn't find my way out. "What do I do?" I said, but Dean and Marylou were asleep. I turned and went slowly back through the town. Outside the town I suddenly saw two car lights coming toward me.

"I'm on the wrong side of the road!" I thought, and moved right, into the mud. I rolled back on to the road and, at the last moment, realized that the *other driver* was on the wrong side, and didn't know it. I pulled the car over into the mud again, and the other car stopped. There were four men inside it, all drunk.

"Which way to Houston?" shouted the driver.

I pointed my thumb back. Suddenly I thought, "They did this on purpose just to ask the way!" They looked sadly at the floor of their car, where empty bottles rolled, then drove away. I started the car; it was stuck in mud a foot deep.

"Dean, wake up," I said. "We're stuck in the mud."

"What happened?" asked Dean, and I told him. He swore, and we put on old shoes and got out into the rain. We woke up Marylou and she sat in the driver's seat while Dean and I pushed

38

from behind. In a minute we were covered with mud. Then suddenly the Hudson slid wildly across the road, and Marylou stopped it, and we got in.

I fell asleep, and the mud on my clothes was hard when I woke up in the morning. We were near Fredericksburg, and it was snowing. I began to wish that I was back in New Orleans. Marylou was driving, and Dean was sleeping. She drove with one hand, the other reaching back to me in the back seat, and made sweet promises about San Francisco. I wanted her, but I was unhappy about it too.

At ten o'clock, Marylou let me drive. Dean slept for hours. I drove several hundred miles across snowy roads. At Sonora, I stole bread and cheese from a store while the owner talked to a big farmer in another corner. Dean was pleased. He was hungry, but we didn't dare spend any money on food.

Dean drove the rest of the way across Texas, about five hundred miles, to El Paso. He stopped once to take off all his clothes, then drove on. "Now Sal, now Marylou," he said. "I want you to do the same. Let the sun shine on your pretty skins. Come on!" Marylou took off her clothes, and so did I. All three of us sat in the front seat. Every mile or two big trucks went by, and the drivers stared as they saw a beautiful girl sitting between two men – all without clothes.

We came into El Paso that evening.

"We have to get some money for gas," Dean said, "or we won't get to San Francisco."

We tried the travel office where you go for share-the-gas rides. We went to the Greyhound bus station to try to persuade somebody to give us their ticket money and travel with us, instead of taking a bus to the Coast. Suddenly, a crazy young kid joined us, and he and Dean rushed out for a beer.

"Come on, man, let's go and hit somebody on the head and get his money," the kid said.

"OK, kid!" shouted Dean. They ran off. For a moment I was worried, but Dean only wanted to have fun with the kid. They weren't going to hit anybody. Marylou and I waited in the car. She put her arms around me.

"Wait until we get to San Francisco!" I told her.

"I don't care," she said. "Dean's going to leave me."

"When are you going back to Denver?" I asked.

"I don't know. I don't care. Can I go back east with you?"

"We'll have to get some money in San Francisco," I said.

"I know a restaurant where you can get a job," she said, "and I can be a waitress. I know a hotel where we can stay. We'll stay together. Oh, I'm sad."

"What are you sad about, kid?" I said.

"Everything," she said. "I wish Dean wasn't so crazy."

Dean came back, laughing. "He was a crazy kid!" he said, and he jumped in the car and drove fast out of El Paso. "We'll just have to pick up some hitch-hikers."

We saw one outside El Paso – a kid about seventeen years old – and Dean stopped. "How much money do you have?" asked Dean. The kid had no money, but Dean told him to get in the car anyway. His name was Alfred.

Then I remembered my old friend Hal Hingham in Tucson, Arizona. "He'll lend me five dollars," I said. Immediately Dean said that we were going to Tucson.

We arrived in Arizona at dawn. I woke up to find everybody asleep in the car. I got out. We were in the mountains – cool purple airs, red mountainsides, green valleys, and a beautiful sunrise. It was time for me to drive on. I pushed Dean and the kid out of the way, and went down the mountain with the engine off to save gas. I asked the man at the gas station in Benson, "Do you know a store where I can sell my watch?" And he pointed to a store near the station. The watch was a birthday present from Rocco and the man in the store gave me a dollar for it, and I went back to the gas station.

Now we had enough gas to get us to Tucson, and Dean drove there. The downtown streets were busy, the people were wild, ambitious, and happy. We saw Hingham, the writer, at his house in Fort Lowell Road. He was in Arizona to write his book in peace. His wife and baby were with him, and his mother lived across the yard in her own house. Hingham had heard of Dean through letters from New York. Hingham was wearing an old coat and was smoking a pipe. His mother invited us into her kitchen to eat. Then Hingham gave me five dollars. He was a sad, lonely man who wanted to get back to New York.

Us? We wanted to get to San Francisco – and we were nearly there!

Chapter 12   Goodbyes

The wonderful white city of San Francisco was in front of us –
there on its eleven hills, with the blue Pacific Ocean and its
moving wall of fog beyond.

"There she is!" shouted Dean. "We got here! Just enough gas!
We can't go any further because there's no more land! Now
Marylou, you and Sal go immediately to a hotel and wait for me
to contact you in the morning, as soon as I've made definite
arrangements with Camille."

And he drove on to the Oakland Bay Bridge and it carried us
in. The downtown office buildings were just putting on their
lights. We got out of the car on O'Farrell Street, and the smell of
Chinese cooking floated in the air. We took all our things out of
the car.

Suddenly Dean was saying goodbye. He wanted to see Camille
and find out what had happened. Marylou and I watched him
drive away. "You see what a pig he is?" said Marylou. "Dean will
leave you whenever it suits him!"

We eventually got a hotel room, then about midnight we
warmed up a tin of pork and beans and ate them. I looked out of
the hotel window at the lights.

Marylou and I lived together for two days in the hotel. She
wasn't really interested in me, and we argued a lot. We also spent
whole nights in bed together. One night she disappeared with a
nightclub owner. I had an appointment with her, and was waiting
for her across the street from an expensive apartment house.
Suddenly she came out with her girlfriend, the nightclub owner,
and a rich old man. She had gone to see her girlfriend, but now I
saw what a prostitute she was. She saw me but did not make any
sign, and they all got into a Cadillac car and drove off.

42

I walked around, picking up cigarettes from the street, then went back to the hotel room. From the window of the room I smelled all the food of San Francisco. There were seafood places out there, where the bread was hot, and the baskets were good enough to eat too. There were places where they cooked thick red roast beef, or chicken. There were places where they cooked hamburgers, and where the coffee was cheap. Oh, and the smell of Chinese food cooking . . .

Dean finally found me when he decided that I was worth saving. He took me home to Camille's house.

"Where's Marylou?" he said.

"She ran away," I said.

I rested for a few days in Camille's house. You could see all of San Francisco's green and red lights in the rainy night from her living-room window in Liberty Street. One morning Dean stood by that window without his clothes on, and watched the sunrise.

He got a job trying to sell stoves, but he didn't sell any. At night we went to clubs and listened to wild jazz music. Then I received some money from my aunt, and I got ready to go back home.

Why did I come to San Francisco? I don't know. Camille wanted me to leave; Dean just didn't care. I bought some bread and made sandwiches to take with me on the road. The last night Dean went crazy and found Marylou somewhere downtown, and we got in the car and drove all over Richmond to jazz clubs and bars.

At dawn I got on my New York bus and said goodbye to Dean and Marylou. They wanted some of my sandwiches, but I said, "No." It was a sad and gloomy moment. We were all thinking that we were not going to see one another again, and we didn't care.

43

Chapter 13 Back in San Francisco

In the spring of 1949 I had saved a few dollars and I went to Denver. I thought about living there, but I was lonely. Nobody was there – no Babe Rawlins, Ray Rawlins, Tim Gray, Betty Gray, Roland Major, Dean Moriarty, Carlo Marx, Ed Dunkel, nobody. I worked for a while in the fruit market – the hardest job of my whole life. In the evenings I walked in the dark, mysterious streets. I went to see a rich girl I knew and spent the night with her. In the morning she gave me a hundred dollars. "You've talked about a trip to San Francisco," she said. "Take this money and go have your fun." So all my problems were solved, and I got a share-the-gas ride with four other fellows.

Soon I was seeing the city of San Francisco again, in the middle of the night. I immediately wanted to see Dean. He had a little house now, and I knocked on his door at two o'clock in the morning.

"Sal!" he cried, when he opened the door. "You've finally come to *me*. I didn't think that you would actually do it."

"Yes," I said. "How are things with you?"

"Not very good," he said. "But we have a million things to talk about, Sal. Come in, come in!"

We began to talk excitedly in the kitchen downstairs, which started Camille crying upstairs. Dean had been quiet for a few months, but now I was here and suddenly he was going mad again.

"She cries, and gets angry every time I'm late, and then won't talk to me when I stay home." He ran upstairs to calm her, and I heard Camille shout, "You're lying!"

Their house had four rooms and a view of the sea. Dean had no car now, and their second baby was coming. It was horrible listening to Camille crying, and later we went out to buy beer and brought it back to the house. Camille finally went to sleep, or spent the night staring into the darkness.

After I left San Francisco the last time, Dean had been crazy about Marylou again, and spent nights standing outside her apartment where every night she entertained a different sailor. He looked through the window in the mornings and saw her in bed with a boy. But he loved her and followed her around town. Then one day he bought some bad marijuana, by mistake, and smoked too much of it. And he had terrible dreams, and woke up screaming.

"Camille was away with the baby, visiting her family," Dean told me. "The neighbors were worried. They sent for a doctor. Then, Sal, I ran to Marylou with some of that marijuana. And do you know that the same thing happened to her? The same terrible dreams. Then I knew I loved her so much that I wanted to kill her. I got a gun and ran to Marylou's house, and she was sleeping with a guy. I went away and came back again, and she was alone. I went in and gave her the gun and told her to kill me. She held the gun in her hand for a long time. I said, 'One of us has to die' and she said 'No,' so I beat my head on the wall. Man, I was crazy! And then she calmed me."

"Then what happened?" I asked.

"That was months ago. She finally married a man who sells cars. He has promised to kill me if he ever finds me near her. If necessary, I'll have to kill him, and then I'll go to San Quentin prison." He showed me his hand and I saw that it was injured. "I hit Marylou the last time we met, and I broke my thumb. A horrible doctor tried to mend it, but a pin went through the top of my thumb and infected the bone. I had to have an operation, and a piece off the end of my thumb." He unwrapped the bandages and showed me. "It got worse, and I can't work with it. So I look after the baby while Camille works. You'll see my beautiful little daughter tomorrow, Sal, and I *know* everything will be all right.

"We're growing older, Sal," he went on. "We're beginning to know things. I understand what you tell me about your life, and now you're ready to meet a girl, and make her your own . . . I've tried so hard with my women, Sal!"

And in the morning Camille threw both of us out. I had been out to a bar and I came back to find Dean and Camille shouting at each other. I went through and locked myself in the bathroom. A few moments later Camille threw Dean's things on to the living-room floor and told him to pack. I heard Dean's crazy laugh, together with the cries of the baby, and then he was packing his things into an old suitcase. I got my bag and packed it as Camille lay in bed shouting "You're lying! You're lying!" Then we ran out of the house and down the street.

Dean had not shaved, his hair was wild, and he was wearing a torn shirt. And he was grinning the silliest grin I've ever seen.

"Why did she throw you out?" I said. "What did you do?"

"What?" he said, confused. "What? What?" Poor, poor Dean – half-crazy, with an infected thumb, and surrounded by the broken suitcases of his life across America. "Let's walk to New York," he said, "and consider our circumstances on the way."

I took out my money, counted it, and showed it to him. "I have eighty-three dollars so, yes, let's go to New York – and after that let's go to Italy." His eyes became excited, and I went on, "I'll get a thousand dollars for my book. We'll go and enjoy all the crazy women in Rome, Paris, all those places. We'll sit in pavement cafes!"

We promised ourselves two days of fun in San Francisco before starting our journey, and we went to see Galatea Dunkel about a place to sleep.

Ed had left her again and was in Denver. "He'll come back when his money is gone," she said. "He can't look after himself without me. He's a fool. All he has to do is know that I love him."

We decided to go out that night and listen to some jazz, and the three of us went to get Marie, a six-foot blonde who lived in an apartment down the street. She had a little daughter, and an old car which Dean and I had to push down the street before it started.

We went back to Galatea's apartment with Marie and her daughter. Roy Johnson and Dorothy, his wife, came and sat with us.

"Camille called and said that you left her, Dean," Galatea said. "Don't you realize you have a daughter?"

"He didn't leave her," I said. "She kicked him out!"

They all looked at me, particularly Dorothy Johnson who stared at me with a nasty look on her face.

"I think Marylou was very wise to leave you, Dean," said Galatea. "You have no sense of responsibility. You've done so many awful things I don't know what to say to you."

Dean just laughed. He stood on the carpet in the middle of them and did a little dance.

"Camille is crying her heart out tonight," Galatea went on, "but she never wants to see you again. But you don't care! You just stand here and do silly dances!"

Dean did care, and I wanted to go and put my arm around him and tell them that this guy had troubles too.

"Now you're going East with Sal!" said Galatea. "Camille has to stay home and look after the baby now that you've gone. How can she keep her job? And if you see Ed along the road, you tell him to come back or I'll kill him!"

Dean was standing by the door, looking into the street. And then, without speaking a word, he walked out of the apartment and went to wait for us downstairs.

"Come on, Galatea, Marie, let's go to the jazz clubs and forget it," I said. "Dean will be dead one day. Then what can you say to him?"

Chapter 14 The Road Is Life

My stay in San Francisco had lasted just a little more than sixty hours. Now Dean and I were going East again. The car we were traveling in belonged to a tall, thin guy who was on his way home to Kansas. He drove with extreme care. There were two other passengers, a man and a woman – tourists, who wanted to sleep everywhere.

Dean drove after Sacramento, and we traveled fast and crazy, which frightened the others in the car. We left Sacramento at dawn and were crossing the Nevada desert by noon. It was a hot, sunny afternoon, and all the towns along the Nevada road rolled by one after another. By the evening we could see the lights of Salt Lake City almost a hundred miles away across the flat country. Suddenly Dean stopped the car and fell back in the corner of the seat. I looked at him and saw that he was asleep.

The people in the back seat sighed and began whispering together. I heard one say, "We can't let him drive any more, he's absolutely crazy."

"He's not crazy," I said. "He'll be all right. And don't worry about his driving, he's the best driver in the world." I sat back and enjoyed the quietness of the desert, and waited for Dean to wake up again.

The tourists insisted on driving the rest of the way to Denver. We sat in the back and talked. But they got tired in the morning and Dean got back into the driver's seat. He drove all the way to Denver, passing everybody and not stopping, and it was good to get out of the car in the city and leave these silly people behind. We still had a long way to go, but it didn't matter. The road is life.

We went to stay with the family who had been my neighbors

when I was in Denver two weeks earlier. The mother was a wonderful woman who drove coal trucks in winter to make money to feed her kids. Her husband left her years before when they were traveling around the country. Her children were wonderful too. The eldest was a boy, who wasn't there that summer. Next was lovely thirteen-year-old Janet, who picked flowers in the fields and wanted to be an actress in Hollywood. Then there were the little ones, Jimmy and Lucy. And they had four dogs.

I warned Dean not to touch Janet. The woman – Frankie, everyone called her – liked Dean straight away. She said that he reminded her of her husband. "And he was a crazy one, I'm telling you!" she said.

There was lots of beer-drinking, and singing. Frankie was about to buy an old car, but Dean immediately made himself responsible for choosing it. This was because he wanted to use it himself to pick up college girls and take them up into the mountains. But Frankie was afraid to spend her money when they got to the garage. Dean sat down on the pavement and beat his head with his hands.

"You *can't* get anything better for a hundred dollars!" he shouted. And he swore until his face was purple.

Next day we went to downtown Denver to see the travel office for a car to New York. Later, on the way to Frankie's, Dean suddenly went into a sports store, calmly picked up a ball, and came out again. Nobody noticed. Nobody ever notices things like this. It was a hot, sleepy afternoon and we played "catch" as we walked along. "Don't worry, we'll get a travel-office car tomorrow," said Dean.

We started drinking a big bottle of whisky at Frankie's house. A beautiful young girl lived across the field at the back of the house. As we drank the whisky, Dean ran out of the kitchen door and across the field to throw stones at her window and to whistle to her. Suddenly he came back, his face pale. "The girl's mother is coming after me with a gun, and she got a gang of college kids from down the road to beat me."

"Where are they?" I said.

"Across the field," said Dean. He was drunk. We went out together and I saw groups of people on the road.

"Here they come!" somebody shouted.

"Wait a minute," I said. "What's the matter, please?"

The mother was there, with a big gun across her arm. "Your friend has annoyed us for long enough. If he comes back here again I'm going to shoot and kill him," she said.

I was so drunk I didn't care either, but I calmed everybody a little. "He won't do it again," I said. "He's my brother, and he listens to me. Put your gun away."

Dean swore quietly as the girl watched from her bedroom window. I took Dean back across the field.

"Whooee!" he shouted. "I'm going to get drunk tonight!"

Frankie wanted to go to a bar and drink beer, and the three of us went out in a taxi to a place outside the town, near the hills. After a few drinks, Dean ran out and stole a car that was parked outside. He drove to downtown Denver and came back with a newer, better one. Suddenly I saw cops and people outside, talking about the stolen car.

"Somebody's been stealing cars!" a cop was saying.

Dean was right behind the cop, saying, "Oh, yes, yes." Then he came inside and had another drink, and said, "I'm going out to get a really good car this time, and go for a big drive into the mountains." And he ran out, jumped into the nearest car, and drove away. Nobody noticed him. A few minutes later he was back in a different car, a new one.

"It's a beautiful car," he whispered. "Let's all go riding."

"I'm not going out in a stolen car," I told him.

So he ran out of the bar and drove away.

Frankie and I got a taxi to take us home. Suddenly, Dean went past us in the stolen car at ninety miles an hour. Then he turned and rushed back toward the town again as we got out of the taxi. We waited in the dark yard, worried, and a few moments later he returned with yet another car – an old one. He stopped it outside the house, rolled out, went straight into the bedroom, and fell on the bed.

I had to wake him up again to help me start the car. We got into it together, then drove it half a mile and left it under a tree. We got back into the house and Dean went straight to sleep. The living-room was a mess! Beer bottles everywhere. I tried to sleep.

Chapter 15   Driving East

In the morning, Dean went to find the car again. "I want to see if it will carry us East," he said. He came back looking pale. "That's a detective's car and every police station in town knows my fingerprints. I must get out of town fast."

We started packing, and I kissed Frankie and apologized.

"He's a crazy guy," she said. "Just like my husband."

Every minute we expected to see a police car appear outside the door. We said goodbye and hurried off along the road with our bags.

We were lucky at the travel office. They wanted someone to drive a Cadillac – a beautiful big car – to Chicago. The owner had been driving up from Mexico with his family, and he got tired and put them all on a train.

We had to wait an hour for the car, and I fell asleep under a tree. Dean went into town and chatted to a waitress in a cafe. He promised to take her for a ride in his Cadillac later, and then he came back to wake me up with the news.

The Cadillac arrived and Dean immediately drove off with it "to get gas." The travel-office man said, "When's he coming back? The passengers are all ready to go." He pointed to two college boys who were waiting with their suitcases on a seat.

"He just went for gas," I said. "He'll be back."

I ran to the corner and saw Dean waiting for the waitress who was changing her clothes in her hotel room. A moment later she ran out and jumped into the Cadillac. They went to a car park, he told me later, and made love in the back of the car. Then Dean persuaded her to come to New York by bus later that week. Her name was Beverley.

Dean arrived back at the travel office thirty minutes later.

52

"I thought you'd stolen that Cadillac," the travel-office man said to him. "Where were you?"

"I'm responsible for the car, don't worry," I said, because everybody was looking at Dean and guessed that he was crazy. Then Dean began helping the college boys with their luggage, and moments later we were rushing away from Denver at 110 miles an hour.

"The reason we're going northeast, Sal," Dean said as he was driving, "is because we absolutely must visit Ed Wall's farm in Sterling. We can still get to Chicago long before the Cadillac owner's train gets there."

We turned off the highway on to a dirt road that took us across East Colorado. It was raining and the mud was wet and slippery. Dean slowed down to seventy miles an hour.

"You're still going too fast," I said when he turned left and the big car began to slip on the wet road. A moment later the back of the car was in a ditch and the front was on the road. I was angry and disgusted with Dean and I swore. He said nothing, but began to walk to a farmhouse a quarter of a mile up the road, in the rain.

"Is he your brother?" asked the boys in the back seat. "He's a devil with a car, isn't he?"

"He's mad," I said, "and yes, he's my brother."

Dean came back with the farmer in his truck, and the man used some rope and pulled us out of the ditch. The car was muddy brown and some of the front was broken.

We drove away, slower now, until it was dark and Ed Wall's farm was straight in front of us. We saw the light in Mrs. Wall's Kitchen.

Wall was about our age, and tall. He and Dean used to stand around on street corners and whistle at girls. Now he took us into his gloomy brown living-room.

His young wife prepared a wonderful meal for us in the big

farm kitchen. She was a blonde, but like all women who live in the country she complained that her life was boring. Dean pretended that I owned the Cadillac, and that I was a very rich man and he was my driver and my friend.

"Well, I hope you boys get to New York," said Ed. He was sure that Dean had stolen the Cadillac. We stayed at the farm for about an hour, then we were driving off again.

That night I saw the whole of Nebraska unroll before my eyes. We went straight through sleeping towns, and no traffic, in the moonlight. I went to sleep at last and woke up to the dry, hot July Sunday morning in Iowa.

A mad guy in a new Buick car decided to race us. He went past, and we went after him like a big bird. "Now watch," said Dean. He let the Buick get some distance away, then caught up with it. Mad Buick went crazy, and took terrible risks to stay in front. We raced for eighty miles before the mad guy gave up and turned into a gas station. We waved and laughed as we went by him.

We stopped for breakfast at a cafe, then went on again.

"Dean, don't drive so fast now," I said.

"Don't worry," he said. The car was going 110 miles an hour again. My eyes ached and I wanted to get out.

"I'm going in the back seat," I told Dean. "I can't watch the road any more."

He laughed as I jumped into the back seat. One of the boys jumped into the front. I tried to sleep, but I couldn't.

By the afternoon we reached Illinois, and another narrow bridge. Two cars in front of us were moving slowly over it. A very large truck was coming the opposite way, but by the time it got to the bridge the other cars would be over. There was absolutely no room on the bridge for the truck and any cars going in the other direction. The road was crowded and everybody was waiting to pass. Dean came down on all this at 110 miles an hour and never hesitated. He started to pass the slow cars, almost hit the left side of the bridge, went straight on into the shadow of the moving truck, turned right quickly and just missed the truck's left front wheel, almost hit the first slow car, pulled out to pass, and just missed another car that came out from behind the truck to look. It all took just a few seconds, then Dean raced on, leaving a cloud of dust behind us.

We drove into Chicago that evening, the smell of fried food and beer in the air, bright lights all around us.

"We're in the big town, Sal! Whooee!" cried Dean.

We parked the Cadillac, then followed the college boys to a small hotel where they got a room and allowed us to use their shower, and to rest for an hour. Then we said goodbye to those boys, who were glad they had got to Chicago in one piece.

Dean and I went to a bar and listened to some jazz music. And when the musicians moved on to a nightclub, we followed them. They played until nine o'clock in the morning, and Dean and I listened. We rushed out now and then in the Cadillac and tried to find girls, but they were frightened of our big, muddy, scarred car. Dean drove crazily, and soon there were more scars on the car, and the brakes stopped working. Now he couldn't stop at red traffic lights, and the car was a wreck. But "Whooee!," who cared? The musicians were still playing.

At 9 a.m., everybody came out of the club into the Chicago day, ready to sleep till it was night again. It was time for Dean and I to return the Cadillac to the owner, who lived out on Lake Shore Drive in an expensive apartment with a garage underneath. The garage mechanic didn't recognize the Cadillac. We gave him the papers and got out fast. We took a bus back to downtown Chicago, and that was the end of it. We never heard a word from the owner of the Cadillac about the condition of his car, although he had our address and could have complained.

It was time for us to move on, and we took a bus to Detroit.

Dean fell asleep while I made conversation with a lovely country girl who was wearing a low cotton blouse that showed the tops of her beautiful breasts.

"What do you want from life?" I asked her.

She didn't know. She yawned. She was sleepy. She was eighteen, beautiful — and dull.

Dean and I got out of the bus at Detroit. We were tired and dirty, and we went to an all-night movie theater and slept till dawn. We spent most of the morning in bars, chasing girls, and listening to jazz, then went to find our travel-office car. We struggled five miles in a local bus with all our luggage, and got to the home of a man who was going to give us four dollars each for the ride to New York. He was a blond fellow, about fifty, with a wife and kid and a good home. We waited in the yard while he got ready.

The moment we were in the new Chrysler car and off to New York, the poor man realized that he was riding with two madmen. But he soon got used to us.

In the foggy night we crossed Toledo and went on across Ohio. The man got tired near Pennsylvania, so Dean drove the rest of the way to New York and we got there early in the morning.

In an hour, Dean and I were at my aunt's new apartment in Long Island. "Sal," she said, "Dean can stay here a few days, and after that he has to get out, do you understand me?"

That night, Dean and I walked among the railroad bridges and fog lamps of Long Island, and agreed to be friends for ever. Five nights later we went to a party in New York and I met a girl called Inez. I told her I had a friend with me and that she ought to meet him. "Dean!" I called to him. We were both drunk.

An hour later Dean was kneeling on the floor with his chin on her stomach, promising her everything. In a few days they were talking on the telephone with Camille, in San Francisco, arranging for the necessary divorce papers so that they could get married. A few months later Camille had Dean's second baby. And a few months after that, Inez had a baby. Dean now had four children – and no money.

So we didn't go to Italy.

Chapter 16 Together Again in Denver

I sold my book and got some money, then I paid my aunt the rent for the rest of the year. Whenever spring comes to New York, I've got to travel. So for the first time in our lives I said goodbye to Dean in New York and left him there.

"Sal, I wish you weren't going, I really do," he said. "It will be my first time in New York without my old friend. All the time I've been here I haven't had any girl but Inez – this only happens to me in New York!"

"I hope you'll be in New York when I get back," I told him. "I hope, Dean, that some day we'll be able to live on the same street with our families, and get old together."

"That's what I pray for, man, not forgetting all my troubles. I didn't want the new baby but Inez insisted. Did you know Marylou got married to a man who sells cars, and that she's having a baby?" Then he took out a photograph of Camille and her new baby girl. The shadow of a man crossed the child on the sunny pavement.

"Who's that?" I asked.

"Ed Dunkel," said Dean. "He came back to Galatea, and they're in Denver now." He took out other pictures, and I realized that these were photographs our children would look at one day. From these pictures they would guess we had lived smooth, ordinary lives, getting up in the morning to walk proudly on the pavements of life. They would not dream of our wild lives on the road.

I got the Washington bus; wasted some time there, wandering around; went out of my way to see the Blue Ridge, heard the bird of Shenandoah, walked the night streets of Charleston, West Virginia; at midnight, Ashland, Kentucky, and a lonely girl. The dark and mysterious Ohio, and Cincinnati at dawn. Then Indiana fields again, and St. Louis in its great valley clouds of afternoon. By night, Missouri, Kansas fields, and small towns with a sea for the end of every street; dawn in Abilene. East Kansas becomes West Kansas.

Henry Glass was riding on the bus with me. He got on at Terre Haute, Indiana. He had just come out of jail for stealing cars in Cincinnati. He was a twenty-year-old kid with curly hair, and was on his way to live with his brother. The brother and his wife had a job for the kid in Colorado.

When we arrived in Denver we went to a bar and I phoned Tim Gray.

"You?" laughed Tim Gray. "I'm coming now."

In ten minutes he came into the bar with Stan Shephard. They loved Henry and bought him beers. I was back in the soft, dark Denver night, and we started visiting all the bars in town. Stan Shephard had wanted to meet me for years.

"Is it true that you're going to Mexico?" he asked me. "Could I go with you? I can get a hundred dollars, and when I get there I can go to Mexico City College."

OK, it was agreed, Stan was coming with me. He was a tall, shy Denver boy with a big smile who moved slowly and easily. That night, he went to sleep in Henry's hotel room and I stayed at Tim Gray's house. Later on, Babe Rawlins got me a neat little room and we all went there, and had parties every night for a week.

Henry went off to his brother's, and we never saw him again. Tim Gray, Stan, Babe, and I spent a week of afternoons in lovely Denver bars where the waitresses have shy, loving eyes and fall in love with their customers.

I was getting ready to go to Mexico when someone gave me the news. "Sal, guess who's coming to Denver. Dean! He bought a car and is coming out to join you!"

I knew at once that Dean was going mad again. "How can he

send money to either of his wives if he takes all his money out of the bank and buys a car?" I thought.

The news was that he was going to drive me to Mexico.

"Do you think he'll let me come along?" asked Stan.

"I'll talk to him," I said.

I was in Babe's house when Dean arrived. Her mother was away in Europe, and her aunt was living in the house with her. Her aunt was called Charity. She was seventy-five years old and as alert as a bird. She was old but she was interested in everything we said and did, and she shook her head sadly when we drank whisky in the living-room. She sat in her corner, watching us all with her birdy eyes. Babe sat laughing on the couch. Tim Gray, Stan Shephard, and I sat around in chairs.

We were sitting around like this on a sunny afternoon when Dean stopped outside in his old car. He was with Roy Johnson, who had just returned from San Francisco with his wife Dorothy and was living in Denver again. So were Ed and Galatea Dunkel, and Tom Snark. Everybody was in Denver again. I went outside to meet Dean.

"Well, my boy," he said, "I see everything is all right with you. Hello, hello," he said to everybody, and we introduced him to Charity. "Well, Sal, old man, what's the story? When do we leave for Mexico? Tomorrow afternoon? Good. I stopped in Kansas City to see my cousin . . ."

"And Inez?" I asked. "What happened in New York?"

"Officially, Sal, this trip is to get a Mexican divorce, cheaper and quicker than any other kind. Camille agrees at last, and everything is lovely, and we know that we are not now worried about a single thing, don't we, Sal?"

Well, OK, I'm always ready to follow Dean, so we arranged a big night – and it was a night we'll never forget. There was a party at Ed Dunkel's brother's house. Ed looked happy and successful. "Me and Roy are going to go to Denver University," he said. "Listen, Dean gets crazier every year, doesn't he?"

Galatea Dunkel was there. She was trying to talk to someone, but everybody was listening to Dean – Shephard, Tim, Babe, and myself, who all sat side by side in kitchen chairs. Ed Dunkel stood nervously behind him.

Dean was jumping up and down and saying, "Yes, yes! We're all together now and the years have rolled by behind us, and none of us have really changed, and that's so amazing . . ." And on and on. And when we left the party that night and went on to the Windsor bar in one large noisy gang, Dean got more and more drunk.

Dean once lived at the Windsor with his father in one of the rooms upstairs. He wasn't a tourist. He drank in this bar like the ghost of his father; his face got red and sweaty, and he shouted at the bar and rolled across the dance-floor, and tried to play the piano.

There were parties everywhere. There was even a party in a castle where we all drove later – except Dean, who ran off somewhere. Then late in the night it was just Dean and I and Stan Shephard and Tim Gray and Ed Dunkel and Tommy Snark in one car. Stan was happily crazy, and Dean was crazy about Stan. He repeated everything Stan said and wiped the sweat off Stan's face. It was our last night in Denver and we made it big and wild.

Chapter 17 Across the Rio Grande

It was afternoon, and we were driving through Colorado – Dean, Stan, and I. Dean's car was a 1937 Ford, and Stan was riding with his arm hanging over the broken door. He was talking happily when a bug bit him. A few minutes later, his arm began to hurt and get bigger.

We drove on, but Stan's arm got worse.

"We'll stop at the first hospital," I said.

It was dark when we got to Colorado Springs. We passed Walsenburg, Trinidad and then we were in New Mexico. We stopped at a place to get hamburgers, and drove on through the night.

Then Dean was saying, "We'll be in Texas in a few minutes, Sal, and won't be out of it till this time tomorrow, and we won't stop driving."

We reached Amarillo in the morning, and all the way from Amarillo to Childress, Dean and I told Stan the stories of the books we had read. Then at Childress we turned south on to a smaller road to Paducah, Guthrie, and Abilene, Texas. Now Dean had to sleep and Stan and I sat in the front and drove. We stopped south of Abilene to eat on the highway, then went on toward Coleman and Brady, only occasionally passing a house near a thirsty river in the endless heat.

"Mexico's a long way away," said Dean sleepily, from the back seat, "so keep rolling, boys."

I drove to Fredericksburg, where Marylou and I once held hands on a snowy morning in 1949. Where was she now?

Suddenly we were in thick heat at the bottom of a five-mile-long hill, and in front of us were the lights of old San Antonio. Dean came into the front to drive.

"Now, men, listen to me," he said, driving into the town. "We will find a hospital for Stan's arm, and you and I, Sal, will have a good look around these streets. You can see right into the front rooms of the houses, and look at all the pretty daughters sitting around with *True Love* magazines. Whooee! Come on!"

We left Stan at the hospital downtown, then Dean and I went off to look around San Antonio. The air was soft and sweet, and the town was dark and mysterious. Girls in white scarves appeared suddenly in the dark. We saw girls in front rooms, girls under the trees with boys, girls everywhere! Then we rushed back to the hospital where Stan was waiting. He had seen a nurse and said he felt much better, and we put our arms around him and told him everything we'd done.

We were ready for the last 150 miles. I slept in the back of the car till we stopped at a cafe in Laredo at two o'clock in the morning. It was very hot, and we could smell the Rio Grande river. We crossed the Mexican border at three o'clock in the morning and went into Nuevo Laredo. The Mexicans looked lazily at our luggage, then it was time to change our money. Mexicans watched us from under their wide hats in the night. Beyond were music and all-night restaurants with smoke pouring out of the door.

"Welcome to Mexico," a Mexican official said. "Have good time. Watch your money. Watch your driving. Eat good. Don't worry. Is not hard to enjoy yourself in Mexico."

We parked the car and went down the Spanish street into the middle of the dull brown lights. Old men sat on chairs. Nobody actually looked at us, but everybody noticed everything we did. We bought three bottles of cold beer, some Mexican cigarettes, then laughed because our Mexican money could buy so much more than American money. We smiled at everyone. Behind us lay the whole of America, and everything Dean and I knew about life, and about life on the road.

We got back into the car and drove away with one last look at America across the Rio Grande bridge. Immediately we were in the desert and there wasn't a light or car for fifty miles, and all the signs pointed to Mexico City.

"I've got to go there!" said Dean.

We arrived at Sabinas Hidalgo, across the desert, at seven o'clock in the morning, and slowed down to drive through it. A group of girls walked in front of us.

"Where you going, man?" one of them said.

I turned to Dean, amazed. "Did you hear that?"

We stopped for gas the other side of Sabinas Hidalgo, then drove off on the road to Monterrey. Soon we were climbing among cool airs, and could see the big town of Monterrey sending smoke to the blue skies above it. Entering Monterrey was like entering Detroit, among great long walls of factories. We talked about stopping to enjoy the excitements, but Dean wanted to get to Mexico City.

I drove across the hot, flat country till we got to the town of Gregoria. Dean and Stan were asleep in the back of the car. I stopped at a gas station near sunny Gregoria and a kid came across the street and tried to sell me some fruit. "You buy?" he said. "My name Victor."

"No," I said smiling, "I'll buy a girl." Back in San Antonio I had promised to get Dean a girl. It was a joke and a bet.

"OK, OK!" said Victor. "I get you girls."

I woke Dean. "Wake up! We've got girls waiting for us!"

"What? Where?" He jumped up.

"This boy Victor is going to show us where."

"You got any marijuana, kid?" asked Dean.

"Sure," said Victor. "Come with me."

Victor got into the car and we drove to his house the other side of town. A few men were sitting lazily outside.

"Who that?" asked Dean.

"Those my brothers," said Victor. "My mother there too. My sister too. That my family. I'm married. I live downtown." We waited in the car while Victor went to the house and said a few words to an old lady. Victor's brothers smiled at us from under a tree. Later they came across with some marijuana, and we smoked it until it was time for the girls. Then the brothers went back under their tree and we went back into town.

Victor showed us the way to the girls. My head seemed to be going around and around (from the marijuana) and I had to rest it on the seat. I had to struggle to see Dean, and then I could see streams of gold pouring out of the sky and across the roof of the car! It was everywhere!

Later we stopped outside Victor's house and he came across with his little baby. Behind him, too shy to come out of the house, was his little wife. After a minute or two, Victor took the child back to her, climbed back into the car, and we drove off again.

Victor took us to a house in a narrow street – and there were the girls. Some of them were lying on couches across the dance-floor, others were drinking at the bar. Music played loudly, and we began dancing with the girls. People from the town watched us through the windows. Victor wanted a woman, but he was faithful to his wife.

I went with one of the girls to a small square room and we made love. Dean and Stan took girls into other rooms. The afternoon was long and cool. We wanted to stay there, but night was coming.

And we had to get to Mexico City.

Chapter 18 Mexico City

We stopped at Limón to sleep in the car, but it was too hot. Dean got out and put a blanket on the ground to lie on. Stan slept in the front seat with both car doors open. I tried to sleep in the back, but I couldn't, so I climbed up on to the roof and stared up at the black sky.

It was still dark when Dean woke up.

"Let's start the car and get some air!" I cried. "I'm dying of heat!"

We found a gas station, just as the last of the night-bugs threw themselves against the lights and on and around us. I jumped up and down on the pavement. "Let's go!" I shouted.

At dawn we drove up through the mountains and looked down at steaming yellow rivers below. As we climbed, the air got cooler. We passed small Indian houses and children came out to watch us with their big, brown, sad eyes.

The day was long. When evening came, we were near the end of our journey. There were big wide fields on either side of us, and the late sun was turning pink. Then suddenly a short mountain road took us to a place where we could see all of Mexico City below us.

We drove straight down into the center of the town at Reforma. Kids played football in dusty fields. Taxi-drivers overtook us asking, "Do you want girls?" No, we didn't want girls now. Then suddenly we were passing crowded cafes and theaters and many lights.

In downtown Mexico City music came from everywhere. We wandered around in an excited dream, then ate beautiful steaks for half a dollar in a strange Mexican cafe with loud music. The streets were alive all night. Beggars slept wrapped in newspapers;

66

whole families sat on the pavements, playing guitars and laughing in the night. Dean walked through it all with his mouth open and his eyes bright with excitement.

Then I got a fever ... and the next thing I knew I was on a bed, and Dean was looking at me. It was several nights later, and he was leaving Mexico City already.

"Poor Sal," he was saying. "Stan will look after you. Now listen to me if you can in your fever. I got my divorce from Camille and I'm driving back to Inez in New York tonight. I wish I could stay with you. I pray I can come back."

When I opened my eyes again, he was standing with his old broken suitcase looking down at me. I didn't know who he was any more, and he knew this and was sympathetic.

"I've got to go now, Sal," he said. "Goodbye."

When I got better I realized what a rat he was, but then I understood how complicated his life was, how he had to leave me there, sick, to get on with his wives and his troubles. "OK, old Dean, I'll say nothing," I thought.

Chapter 19 The Last Goodbye

When Dean arrived in New York with the divorce papers in his hands, he and Inez immediately got married. And that night he told her that everything was all right and not to worry – and then he jumped on a bus and rushed off across the country to San Francisco to join Camille and the two baby girls. So now he was married three times, twice divorced, and living with his second wife.

In the fall I came home from Mexico City. And one night I was standing in a dark street in Manhattan and I called up to a window where I thought my friends were having a party. But a pretty girl put her head out of the window and said, "Yes? Who is it?"

"Sal Paradise," I said.

"Come on up," she said. "I'm making hot chocolate."

So I went up and there she was, the girl with the pure and innocent eyes I had always searched for. We agreed to love each other madly. Her name was Laura. In the winter we planned to go to San Francisco, and I wrote to Dean and told him. Dean wrote back a long, long letter to say that he was coming to get me, and that he would personally choose the truck to drive us and our furniture home. We had six weeks to save the money for the truck. But then Dean arrived five and a half weeks early, and nobody had any money for the truck.

"Why did you come so soon, Dean?" I asked.

"Oh – so soon, yes." He looked at me strangely. "We – that is, I don't know. Of course, Sal, I can talk as soon as ever, and I have many things to say to you, and we still haven't talked of Mexico and my leaving you there in a fever – but no need to talk. Absolutely, now, yes?" And then he talked crazily for three hours about his trip.

"What about Camille?" I asked him eventually.

"Said OK, of course – waiting for me. Camille and I all straight for ever-and-ever . . ."

"And Inez?"

"I – I want her to come back to San Francisco with me and live the other side of town – don't you think?" He looked puzzled suddenly. "Don't know why I came." Later he said, "Well, yes, of course, I wanted to see your sweet girl and – love you as ever."

He stayed in New York three days. He spent one night with Inez explaining and fighting, and then she threw him out. A letter came for him to me. It was from Camille.

"My heart broke when I saw you go away . . . I want Sal and his friend to come and live in the same street . . . I pray you'll get back safely . . . I can't help worrying . . . dear Dean, it's the end of the first half of the century. Welcome with love and kisses to spend the other half with us. We all wait for you. Signed, Camille, Amy, and Little Joanie."

The last time I saw Dean it was under sad and strange circumstances. Remi Boncœur had arrived in New York after a round-the-world trip, and I wanted him to meet Dean. They did meet, but Dean couldn't talk any more and said nothing. Remi had tickets for a Duke Ellington concert, and insisted that Laura and I went with him and his girl. He had his Cadillac outside, ready to take us.

"Goodbye, Dean," I said. "I wish I didn't have to go to the concert."

"Can I ride to Fortieth Street with you?" he whispered. "Want to be with you as much as possible, and it's so cold here in New York . . ." I whispered to Remi. No, he wouldn't take Dean, he liked me but he didn't like my crazy friend.

So Dean couldn't ride with us, and the only thing I could do was sit at the back of the Cadillac and wave at him. The last I saw of him was when he went around the corner of Seventh Avenue. I had told everything about Dean to Laura, and now she almost began to cry.

"Oh, we shouldn't let him go like this," she said. "What shall we do?"

Old Dean's gone, I thought, then said, "He'll be all right." So off we went to the sad concert, and all the time I was thinking of Dean and how he got back on the train to ride over three thousand miles across the country, and never knew why he had come anyway, except to see me.

So in America when the sun goes down and I sit and watch the long skies over New Jersey and think about the land that rolls away to the West Coast, and all that road, and all the people dreaming on it, I think of Dean Moriarty.

ACTIVITIES

Chapters 1–4

Before you read

1   Find these words in your dictionary. They are all in the story.

   couch   guy   hitch-hiking   kid   jazz   marijuana   pie

   slim   truck

   Which words refer to:

   a types of people?

   b a kind of music?

   c a way of traveling?

   d an illegal drug?

   e a form of transport?

   f a seat?

   g someone's appearance?

   h a kind of food?

2   *On the Road* is a story about traveling. Look at the picture on the cover of the book. What do you think?

   a When does the story take place?

   b How old are the people in the story?

   c Are they rich or poor?

   d Do they have ordinary lives?

After you read

3   Answer these questions:

   a Has Sal Paradise ever been married?

   b Where is Dean when Sal first hears of him?

   c What is Sal doing at the beginning of the book? Does he have a job?

   d Why does Dean come to see Sal in Paterson?

   e What is Sal's "greatest ride"?

   f Who does Sal stay with when he first arrives in Denver?

4   Discuss what you know about Dean Moriarty at this point in the book.

Chapters 5–8

Before you read

5 In this part of the story, Sal describes "a wonderful night." What do you think his idea of a great night is? What is yours?

6 Find these words in your dictionary. Then complete the sentences below.

barracks   broke   cop   highway   prostitute   races

a A ..... stopped us on the ..... because we were driving too fast.

b We went to the ..... and I put all my money on a horse. I lost it all and now I'm ......

c A lot of men were staying at the ..... , sleeping in big, shared rooms.

d His girlfriend had left him and he was in bed with a ......

After you read

7 Who says these words? Who to? What is happening?

a "You've arrived! You finally got on that old road."

b "He came in through the window!"

c "Excuse me, but I don't teach high-school French."

d "We can hitch-hike to my home town, Sabinal, and live in my brother's garage."

e "I bought it. I've worked on the railroads, for four hundred dollars a month."

8 What does Remi ask Lee Ann and Sal to do to help him? Is the event a success?

Chapters 9–12

Before you read

9 What is the purpose of the journey east? How do you think the travelers will finance their trip?

10 Old Bull Lee calls Sal and says, "A girl called Galatea just arrived at my house." Why do you think she is there?

After you read

11 Who:

a is playing at Birdland?

    b drives off the road and into the mud?

    c gives Sal five dollars?

    d says she wants to be with Sal in San Francisco?

    e gets a job selling stoves?

12 Describe the relationships between Sal, Dean, Marylou, and Camille.

Chapters 13–16

Before you read

13 Remember the end of the last chapter, and discuss the questions below.

We were all thinking that we were not going to see one another again, and we didn't care.

    a Why did they feel like that?

    b Will any of them change their minds? Why (not)?

14 Make a connection between these pairs of words. Check the meaning of the words in italics in a dictionary.

    a rainwater – *ditch*   **c** crime – *fingerprint*

    b marriage – *divorce*

After you read

15 Are these sentences true or false? Correct the false ones.

    a A rich girl gives Sal a hundred dollars.

    b Dean kills Marylou.

    c Dean is a careful driver.

    d Dean steals cars.

    e Sal damages the Cadillac.

    f The owner of the Cadillac makes them pay for the damage.

    g Dean becomes a father while he is in New York.

    h Sal travels west alone.

16 Work in pairs. Talk about the way Dean lives his life.

    Student A: You are shocked by his terrible behavior. Express your opinion.

    Student B: You think his behavior is interesting and amusing. Explain why.

Chapters 17–19

Before you read

17 How do you think the story will end?

18 Read this sentence from the story:
    He was talking happily when a bug bit him.
    What do you think a *bug* is? Check in your dictionary.

After you read

19 What is the reason Dean goes to Mexico? How does the story end for him?

20 How does Sal feel when:
    a Dean leaves him in Mexico?
    b he watches Dean walk away in New York?

21 In which year does the book end? What does Camille hope for in the future?

Writing

22 *On the Road* first appeared in 1957. Why do you think it is still popular?

23 Do the characters in the book share any sense of right and wrong? Give reasons for your opinions.

24 Choose one of the people in the story. Write about their character and behavior. Would you like them as your friend?

25 Some people say that *On the Road* is about a journey of self-discovery. In what ways do you think this is true?

Answers for the Activities in this book are published in our free resource packs for teachers, the Penguin Readers Factsheets, or available on a separate sheet. Please write to your local Pearson Education office or to: Marketing Department, Penguin Longman Publishing, 5 Bentinck Street, London W1M 5RN.